This book is a presentation of Weekly Reader Books. Weekly Reader Books offers book clubs for children from preschool through high school. For further information write to: **Weekly Reader Books**, 4343 Equity Drive, Columbus, Ohio 43228.

Published by arrangement with Viking Penguin, a division of Penguin Books USA Inc. Weekly Reader is a federally registered trademark of Field Publications. This Weekly Reader Books edition is printed in the United States of America.

VIKING
Published by the Penguin Group
Viking Penguin, a division of Penguin Books USA Inc.,
40 West 23rd Street, New York, New York 10010, U.S.A.
Penguin Books Ltd, 27 Wrights Lane, London W8 5TZ England
Penguin Books Australia Ltd, Ringwood, Victoria, Australia
Penguin Books Canada Ltd, 2801 John Street, Markham, Ontario, Canada L3R 1B4
Penguin Books (N.Z.) Ltd, 182-190 Wairau Road, Auckland 10, New Zealand

Penguin Books Ltd, Registered Offices: Harmondsworth, Middlesex, England

First published in Great Britain by Methuen Children's Books, 1990
First American edition published 1990

1   3   5   7   9   10   8   6   4   2

Text copyright © Andrew and Diana Davies, 1990
Illustrations copyright © Paul Dowling, 1990
All rights reserved
ISBN 0-670-83321-5

Printed in Belgium by Proost International Book Production

Weekly Reader Children's Book Club Presents

POONAM'S PETS

Story by Andrew and Diana Davies
Pictures by Paul Dowling

Viking

Poonam is in Class One and her teacher is Mrs Wig.

Poonam is a bit on the small side and a bit on the quiet side. In fact you have to put your ear right down by her mouth if you want to hear what she is saying.

"All right, Class One," said Mrs Wig one day. "Be quiet and listen. I have something special to tell you."

"On Friday," said Mrs Wig, "we are going to have a Pets Assembly. That means you can bring your pets to school, and they can go to Assembly." Everybody laughed. It was funny to think of pets in Assembly.

"Now," said Mrs Wig, "how many of you have pets?" Everyone in Class One put up their hands.

"That's a lot of pets," said Mrs Wig. "Let's see what sort of pets we have."

There were dogs
     and cats
     and goldfish
     and rabbits.

Ranjeev put his hand up for everything, but Poonam didn't put her hand up at all.

"All right," said Mrs Wig, "have any of you got . . . . . *giraffes*?"

Only Ranjeev put his hand up.

"Ranjeev," said Mrs Wig, "you can't have a *giraffe*!"

"I have," said Ranjeev. "He's got big brown spots."

"Poonam," said Mrs Wig, "you haven't said anything yet.
What sort of pet have you got?"

Poonam got up very quietly and walked to Mrs Wig's
table, and Mrs Wig put her ear down, and Poonam
whispered into it.

"Poonam's got *lions*," said Mrs Wig to Class One.
Poonam smiled a quiet little smile.

On Friday, all the pets came to the Pets Assembly. Some of them came in cars, some came in boxes, some came in hutches, and some came in cages. Kamaljit's dog came in a baby carriage, because he was an old dog. All the other dogs walked to school on leashes.

The goldfish were very quiet and good. The cats were *quite* well behaved, except for one or two who were making horrible faces at the dogs and spitting at them. Julie's dog Prince wanted to sniff everyone's trousers, and Gurpal's dog Pongo barked all the time and wanted to fight everybody.

"I'm not sure if this Pets Assembly is such a good idea, after all," said Mrs Wig.

Ranjeev came a little bit late, and rather out of breath.
He had a big lump under his sweater.

"What's in there, Ranjeev?" said Gurpal.

"My giraffe," said Ranjeev.

"Looks more like a rabbit to me," said Gurpal.

"It's a giraffe!" shouted Ranjeev. "It's just not grown up yet!"

"I think my dog Pongo would like to eat your giraffe,"
said Gurpal.

It was nearly time for Assembly, and everyone in Class One
was there except Poonam. Mrs Wig looked at the clock.

"Well," said Mrs Wig, "I'm afraid we'll have to start.
Line up quietly please, dogs on the left and cats on the
right." Lining up took quite a long time because some of
the dogs got mixed up. Dogs are not very good at telling left
from right. And then they all went into the hall.

The hall looked beautiful, with the dogs on one side and the cats on the other side. It did not matter where the goldfish sat, because goldfish are very peaceful.

When they saw all the other children looking at their pets, the children in Class One felt very pleased and proud.

And still Poonam had not come.

Mrs Wig went to the front of the hall.
    "Good morning, everybody," she said.
"Welcome to Class One's Special Pets Assembly."

And then something amazing happened.
The door opened, and in came Poonam.
And behind Poonam, walking very quietly,
one behind the other in a row, were . . .

SIX ENORMOUS LIONS!

All the dogs hid under the chairs. The cats opened their eyes wide and stared. They had never seen such big cats before.

Ranjeev's giraffe was very frightened, and burrowed deep under his sweater. The children were frightened as well, and wanted to run out.

Poonam and her six enormous lions walked right to the front of the hall, and the lions sat down in a row, blinking sleepily at the children. They did not look too fierce. They looked solemn and friendly and wise.

Poonam went up to Mrs Wig. Mrs Wig bent her ear down
and Poonam whispered in it. Then Mrs Wig stood up straight.
   "Poonam says we are not to be frightened," she said.
"These are very good lions."

Poonam whispered in Mrs Wig's ear again.

"Poonam says her lions will now do their act for you," said Mrs Wig.

Poonam clapped her hands. Two lions balanced their front paws on chairs while the lions behind stood up on

their back legs, balancing with their paws on each other's shoulders.

They all opened their mouths wide, showing their huge teeth, and Poonam gave each of them a big lion biscuit. All the children clapped and cheered.

The lions sat down in a row again, looking very pleased with themselves.

Poonam whispered to Mrs Wig.

"Ask them yourself, Poonam," said Mrs Wig.
Poonam turned and looked at the children.
Then she said in a very loud voice:

"WOULD ANYBODY LIKE A RIDE ON MY LIONS?"

The children were amazed. No one had ever heard Poonam speak in a loud voice before.
So the whole school went out to the playground and the six enormous lions stood in a row. They were very big, but Poonam and Mrs Wig helped the little ones to get up.

But when it was Ranjeev's turn he stood and looked
at the ground.

"What's the matter, Ranjeev?" said Poonam.
Ranjeev whispered in Poonam's ear.

"What?" said Poonam. "I can't hear you."

"I'm scared," said Ranjeev.

"It's all right," said Poonam. "I'll hold your hand."

Poonam and the six enormous lions stayed all day.
When it was time to go home, Poonam clapped her hands
to the lions. They lined up and Poonam and her six
enormous lions went quietly home.

Poonam is still a bit small, and rather quiet. But when she
has something important to say, she says it in a loud voice.
She never talks about her six enormous lions,
and no one else has ever seen them since the day of
the Pets Assembly.